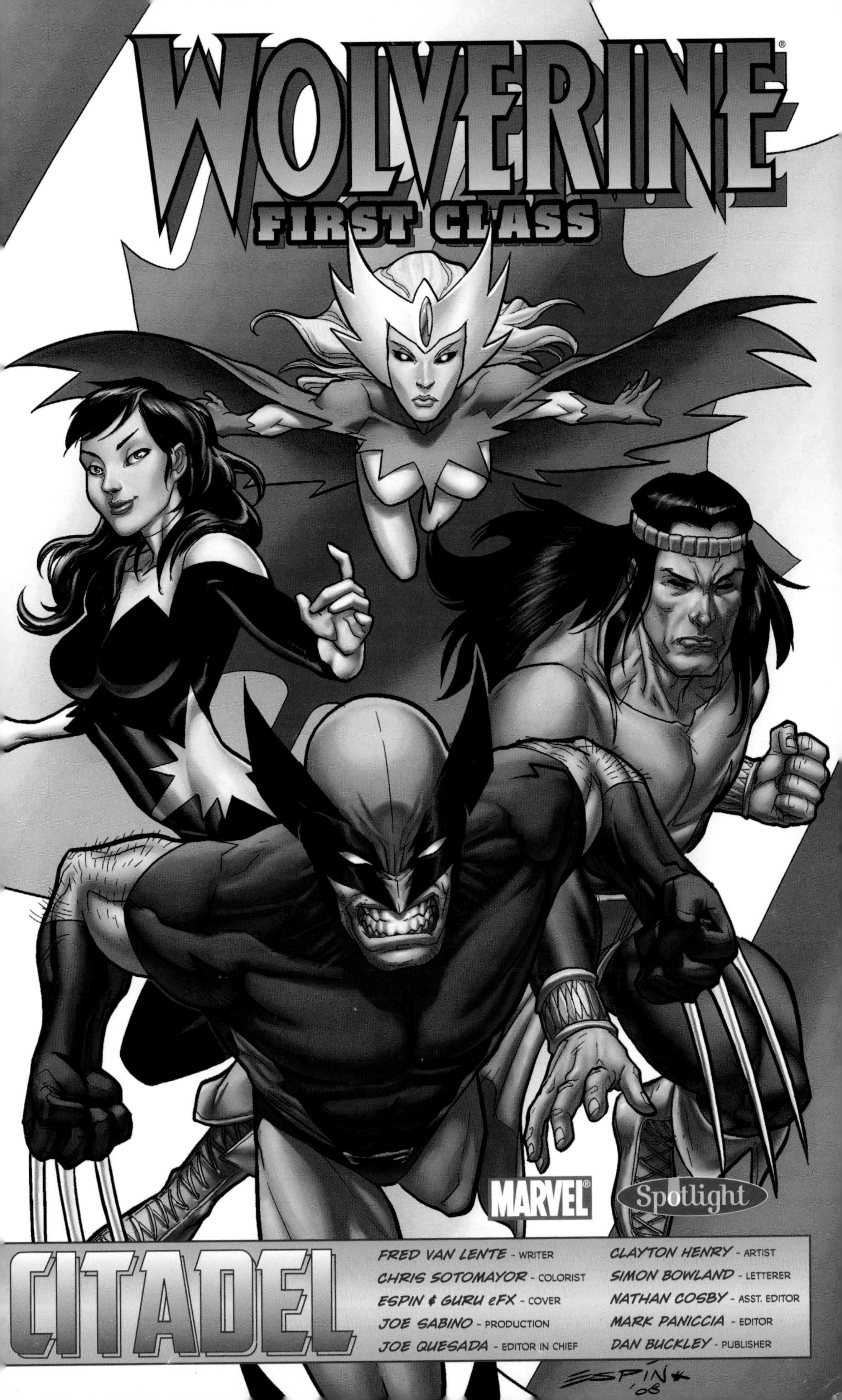
WOLVERINE
FIRST CLASS
MARVEL
Spotlight

CITADEL

FRED VAN LENTE - WRITER
CLAYTON HENRY - ARTIST
CHRIS SOTOMAYOR - COLORIST
SIMON BOWLAND - LETTERER
ESPIN & GURU eFX - COVER
NATHAN COSBY - ASST. EDITOR
JOE SABINO - PRODUCTION
MARK PANICCIA - EDITOR
JOE QUESADA - EDITOR IN CHIEF
DAN BUCKLEY - PUBLISHER

ESPIN '08

VISIT US AT
www.abdopublishing.com

Reinforced library bound edition published in 2010 by Spotlight, a division of the ABDO Group, 8000 West 78th Street, Edina, Minnesota 55439. Spotlight produces high-quality reinforced library bound editions for schools and libraries. Published by agreement with Marvel Characters, Inc.

Printed in the United States of America, North Mankato, Minnesota.
012009
122013

Library of Congress Cataloging-in-Publication Data

Van Lente, Fred.
  Citadel / Fred Van Lente, writer ; Clayton Henry, artist ; Chris Sotomayor, colorist ; Simon Bowland, letterer. -- Reinforced library bound ed.
     p. cm. -- (Wolverine, first class)
  "Marvel."
  ISBN 978-1-59961-670-4
  1. Graphic novels. 2. Graphic novels. [1. Graphic novels. 2. Superheroes--Fiction.] I. Henry, Clayton, ill. II. Sotomayor, Chris. III. Bowland, Simon. IV. Title.
  PZ7.7.V26Ci 2009
  741.5'973--dc22
                          2009010135

All Spotlight books have reinforced library bindings and are manufactured in the United States of

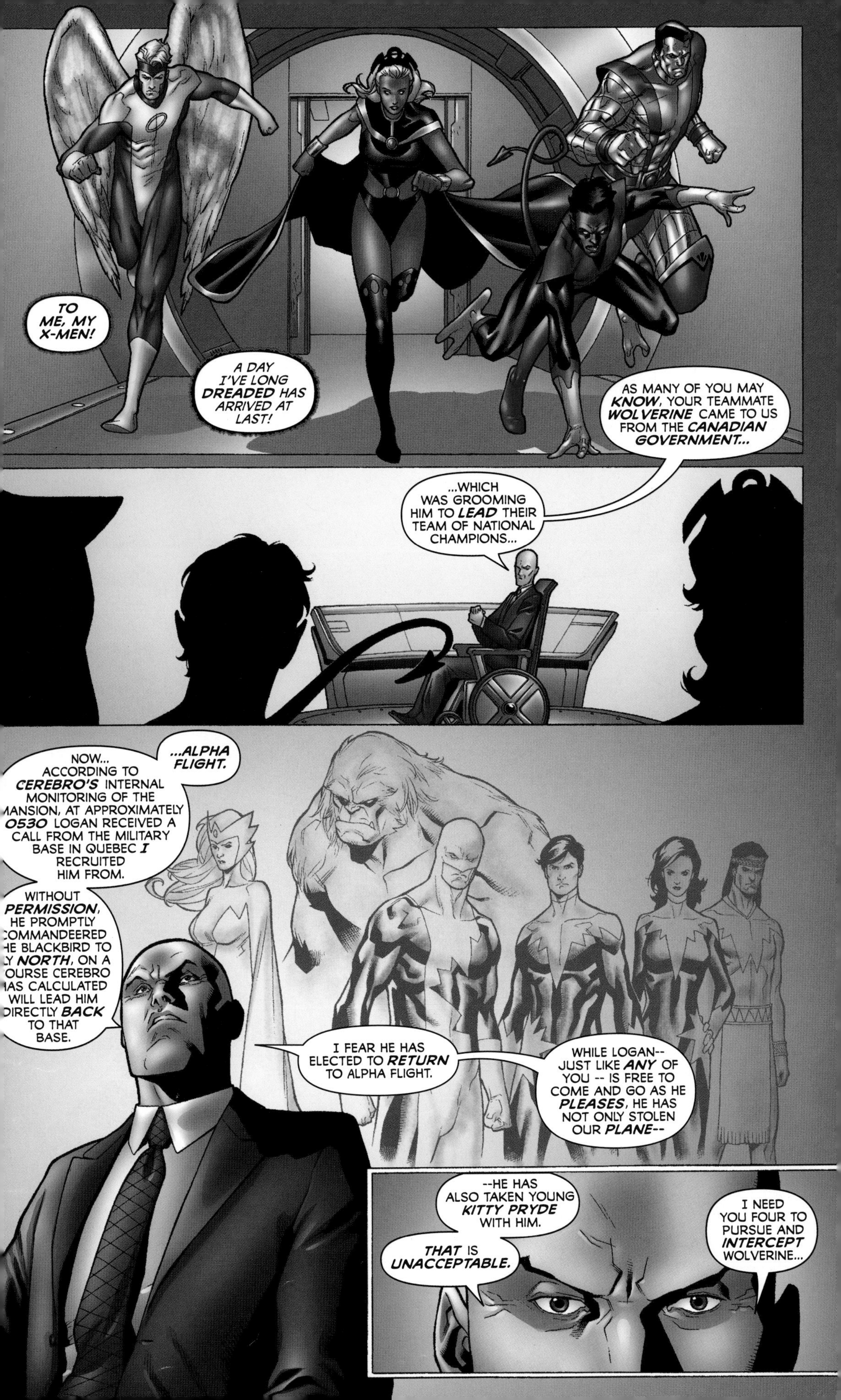

TO ME, MY X-MEN!
A DAY I'VE LONG DREADED HAS ARRIVED AT LAST!
AS MANY OF YOU MAY KNOW, YOUR TEAMMATE WOLVERINE CAME TO US FROM THE CANADIAN GOVERNMENT...
...WHICH WAS GROOMING HIM TO LEAD THEIR TEAM OF NATIONAL CHAMPIONS...
...ALPHA FLIGHT.
NOW... ACCORDING TO CEREBRO'S INTERNAL MONITORING OF THE MANSION, AT APPROXIMATELY 0530 LOGAN RECEIVED A CALL FROM THE MILITARY BASE IN QUEBEC I RECRUITED HIM FROM.
WITHOUT PERMISSION, HE PROMPTLY COMMANDEERED THE BLACKBIRD TO FLY NORTH, ON A COURSE CEREBRO HAS CALCULATED WILL LEAD HIM DIRECTLY BACK TO THAT BASE.
I FEAR HE HAS ELECTED TO RETURN TO ALPHA FLIGHT.
WHILE LOGAN-- JUST LIKE ANY OF YOU -- IS FREE TO COME AND GO AS HE PLEASES, HE HAS NOT ONLY STOLEN OUR PLANE--
--HE HAS ALSO TAKEN YOUNG KITTY PRYDE WITH HIM.
THAT IS UNACCEPTABLE.
I NEED YOU FOUR TO PURSUE AND INTERCEPT WOLVERINE...

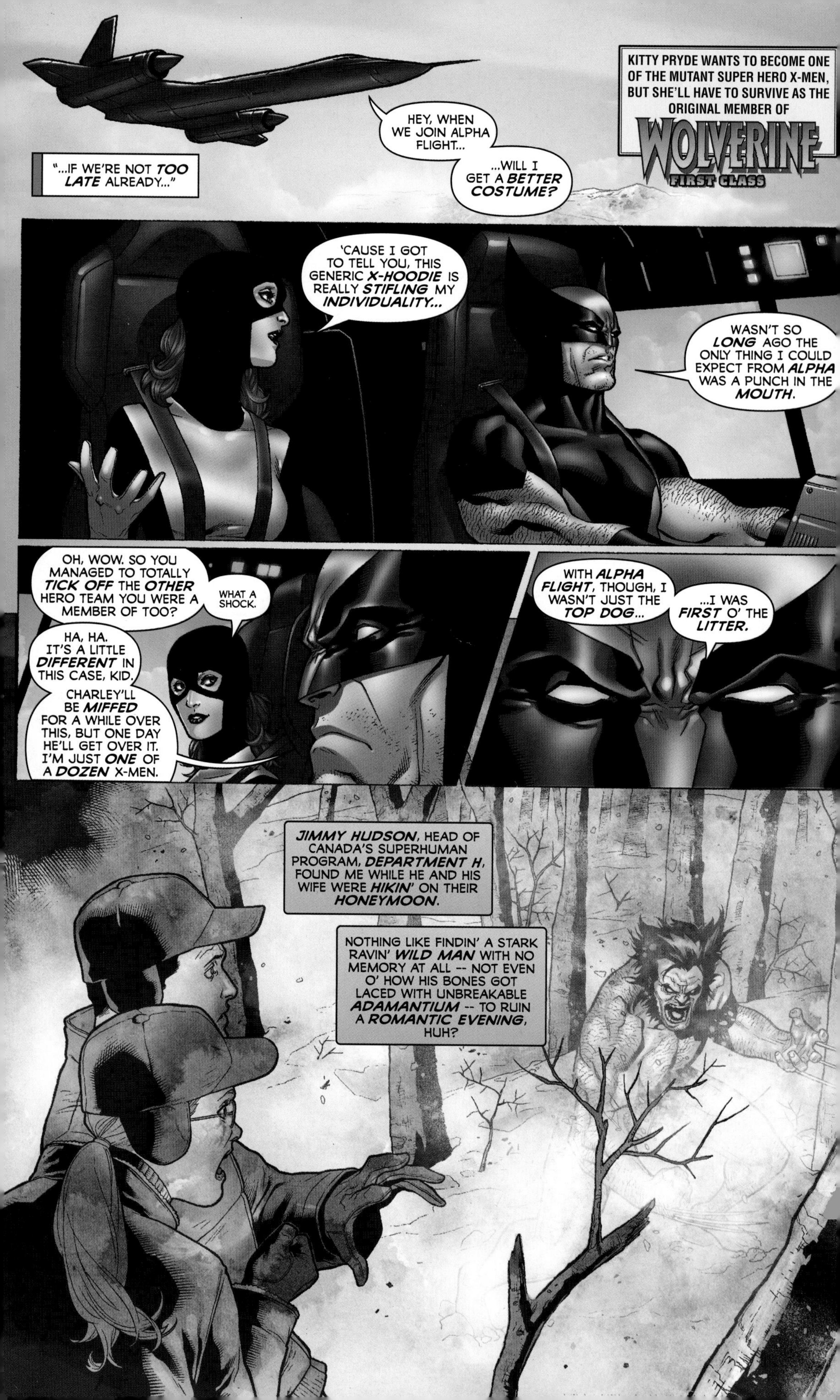
KITTY PRYDE WANTS TO BECOME ONE OF THE MUTANT SUPER HERO X-MEN, BUT SHE'LL HAVE TO SURVIVE AS THE ORIGINAL MEMBER OF
WOLVERINE
FIRST CLASS
"...IF WE'RE NOT TOO LATE ALREADY..."
HEY, WHEN WE JOIN ALPHA FLIGHT...
...WILL I GET A BETTER COSTUME?
'CAUSE I GOT TO TELL YOU, THIS GENERIC X-HOODIE IS REALLY STIFLING MY INDIVIDUALITY...
WASN'T SO LONG AGO THE ONLY THING I COULD EXPECT FROM ALPHA WAS A PUNCH IN THE MOUTH.
OH, WOW. SO YOU MANAGED TO TOTALLY TICK OFF THE OTHER HERO TEAM YOU WERE A MEMBER OF TOO?
WHAT A SHOCK.
HA, HA. IT'S A LITTLE DIFFERENT IN THIS CASE, KID.
CHARLEY'LL BE MIFFED FOR A WHILE OVER THIS, BUT ONE DAY HE'LL GET OVER IT. I'M JUST ONE OF A DOZEN X-MEN.
WITH ALPHA FLIGHT, THOUGH, I WASN'T JUST THE TOP DOG...
...I WAS FIRST O' THE LITTER.
JIMMY HUDSON, HEAD OF CANADA'S SUPERHUMAN PROGRAM, DEPARTMENT H, FOUND ME WHILE HE AND HIS WIFE WERE HIKIN' ON THEIR HONEYMOON.
NOTHING LIKE FINDIN' A STARK RAVIN' WILD MAN WITH NO MEMORY AT ALL -- NOT EVEN O' HOW HIS BONES GOT LACED WITH UNBREAKABLE ADAMANTIUM -- TO RUIN A ROMANTIC EVENING, HUH?

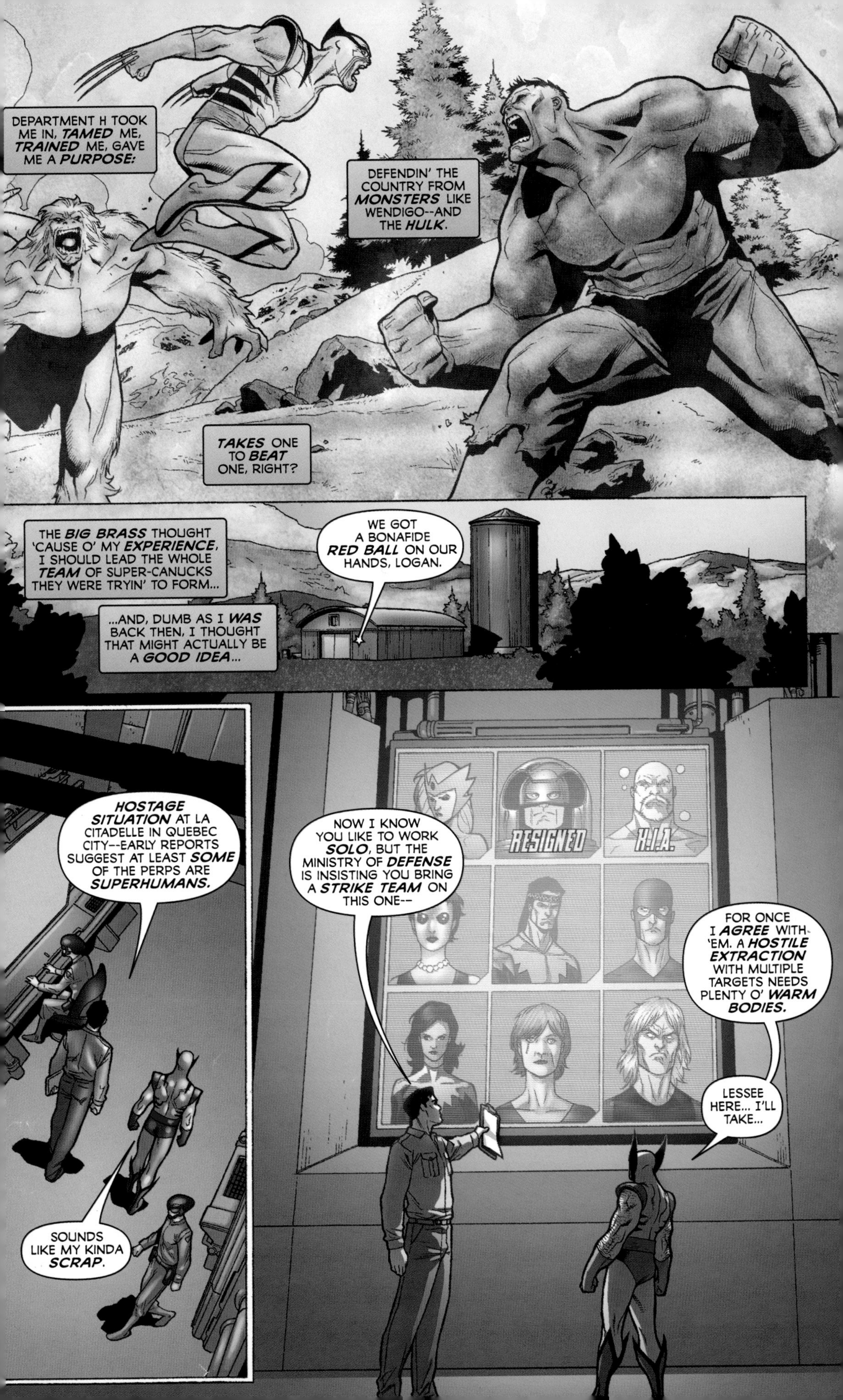
DEPARTMENT H TOOK ME IN, TAMED ME, TRAINED ME, GAVE ME A PURPOSE:
DEFENDIN' THE COUNTRY FROM MONSTERS LIKE WENDIGO--AND THE HULK.
TAKES ONE TO BEAT ONE, RIGHT?
THE BIG BRASS THOUGHT 'CAUSE O' MY EXPERIENCE, I SHOULD LEAD THE WHOLE TEAM OF SUPER-CANUCKS THEY WERE TRYIN' TO FORM...
...AND, DUMB AS I WAS BACK THEN, I THOUGHT THAT MIGHT ACTUALLY BE A GOOD IDEA...
WE GOT A BONAFIDE RED BALL ON OUR HANDS, LOGAN.
HOSTAGE SITUATION AT LA CITADELLE IN QUEBEC CITY--EARLY REPORTS SUGGEST AT LEAST SOME OF THE PERPS ARE SUPERHUMANS.
SOUNDS LIKE MY KINDA SCRAP.
RESIGNED
H.I.A.
NOW I KNOW YOU LIKE TO WORK SOLO, BUT THE MINISTRY OF DEFENSE IS INSISTING YOU BRING A STRIKE TEAM ON THIS ONE--
FOR ONCE I AGREE WITH 'EM. A HOSTILE EXTRACTION WITH MULTIPLE TARGETS NEEDS PLENTY O' WARM BODIES.
LESSEE HERE... I'LL TAKE...

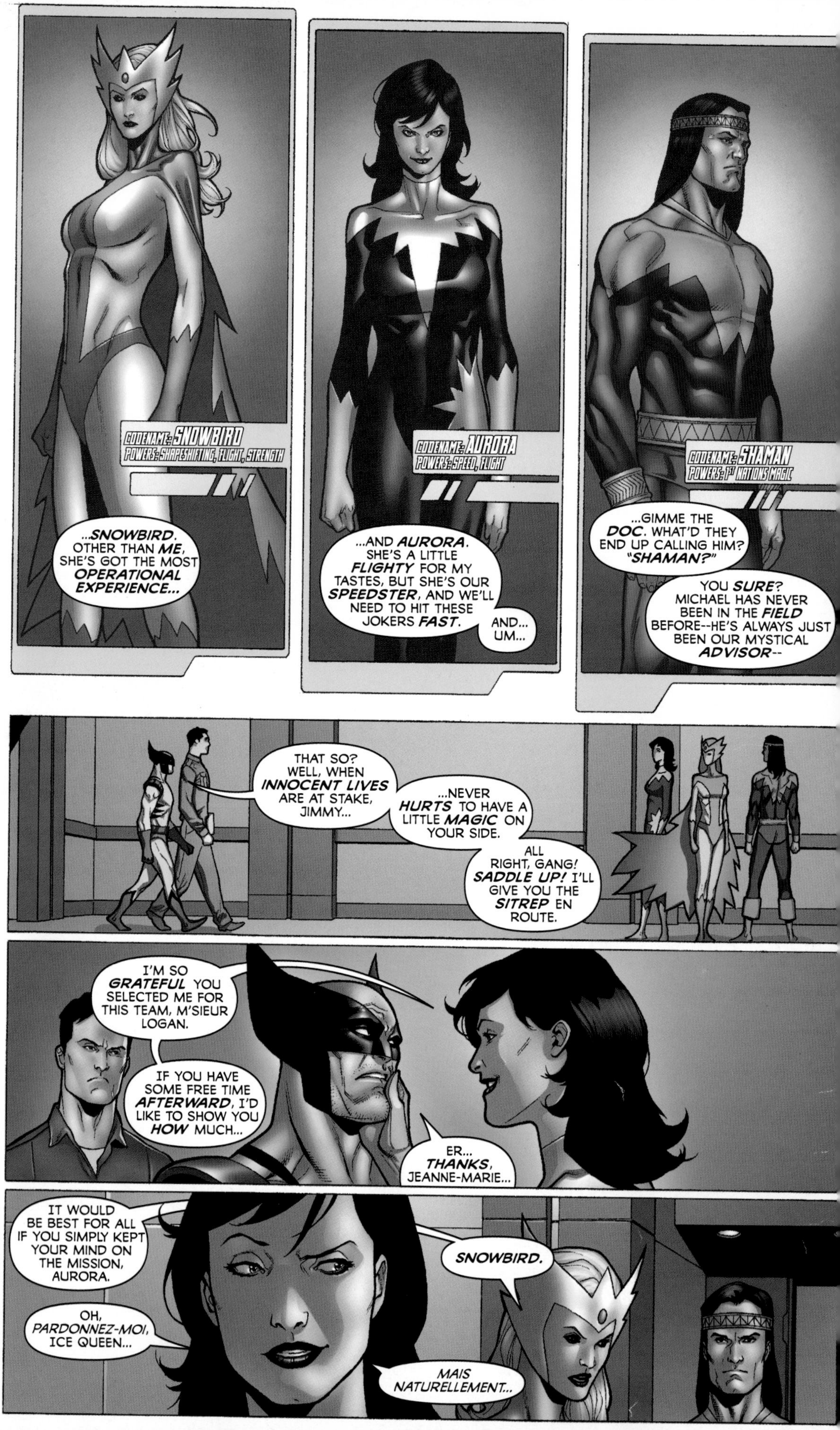

CODENAME: SNOWBIRD
POWERS: SHAPESHIFTING, FLIGHT, STRENGTH
...SNOWBIRD. OTHER THAN ME, SHE'S GOT THE MOST OPERATIONAL EXPERIENCE...
CODENAME: AURORA
POWERS: SPEED, FLIGHT
...AND AURORA. SHE'S A LITTLE FLIGHTY FOR MY TASTES, BUT SHE'S OUR SPEEDSTER, AND WE'LL NEED TO HIT THESE JOKERS FAST.
AND... UM...
CODENAME: SHAMAN
POWERS: 1ST NATIONS MAGIC
...GIMME THE DOC. WHAT'D THEY END UP CALLING HIM? "SHAMAN?"
YOU SURE? MICHAEL HAS NEVER BEEN IN THE FIELD BEFORE--HE'S ALWAYS JUST BEEN OUR MYSTICAL ADVISOR--
THAT SO? WELL, WHEN INNOCENT LIVES ARE AT STAKE, JIMMY...
...NEVER HURTS TO HAVE A LITTLE MAGIC ON YOUR SIDE.
ALL RIGHT, GANG! SADDLE UP! I'LL GIVE YOU THE SITREP EN ROUTE.
I'M SO GRATEFUL YOU SELECTED ME FOR THIS TEAM, M'SIEUR LOGAN.
IF YOU HAVE SOME FREE TIME AFTERWARD, I'D LIKE TO SHOW YOU HOW MUCH...
ER... THANKS, JEANNE-MARIE...
IT WOULD BE BEST FOR ALL IF YOU SIMPLY KEPT YOUR MIND ON THE MISSION, AURORA.
SNOWBIRD.
OH, PARDONNEZ-MOI, ICE QUEEN...
MAIS NATURELLEMENT...

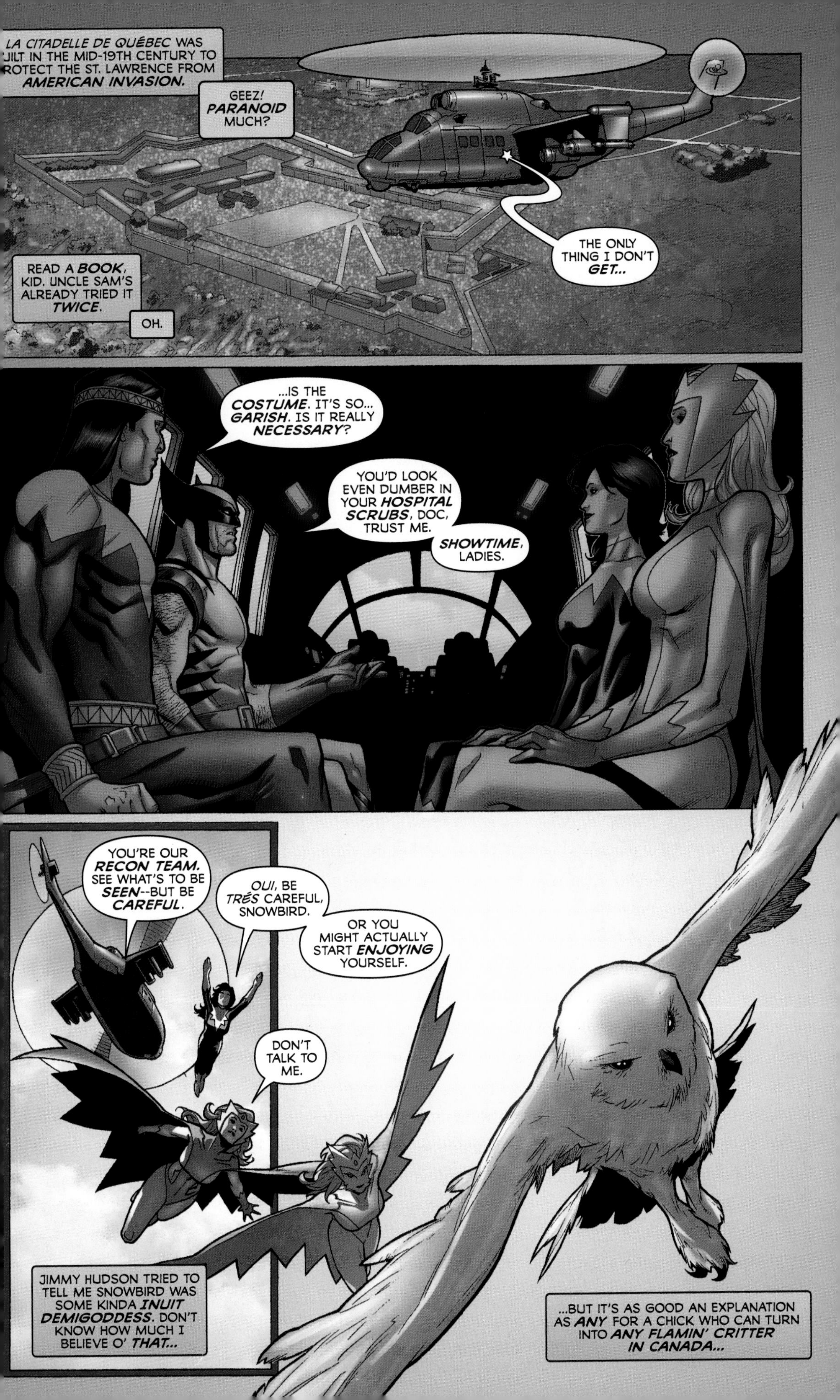
LA CITADELLE DE QUÉBEC WAS UILT IN THE MID-19TH CENTURY TO ROTECT THE ST. LAWRENCE FROM AMERICAN INVASION.
GEEZ! PARANOID MUCH?
THE ONLY THING I DON'T GET...
READ A BOOK, KID. UNCLE SAM'S ALREADY TRIED IT TWICE.
OH.
...IS THE COSTUME. IT'S SO... GARISH. IS IT REALLY NECESSARY?
YOU'D LOOK EVEN DUMBER IN YOUR HOSPITAL SCRUBS, DOC, TRUST ME.
SHOWTIME, LADIES.
YOU'RE OUR RECON TEAM. SEE WHAT'S TO BE SEEN--BUT BE CAREFUL.
OUI, BE TRÉS CAREFUL, SNOWBIRD.
OR YOU MIGHT ACTUALLY START ENJOYING YOURSELF.
DON'T TALK TO ME.
JIMMY HUDSON TRIED TO TELL ME SNOWBIRD WAS SOME KINDA INUIT DEMIGODDESS. DON'T KNOW HOW MUCH I BELIEVE O' THAT...
...BUT IT'S AS GOOD AN EXPLANATION AS ANY FOR A CHICK WHO CAN TURN INTO ANY FLAMIN' CRITTER IN CANADA...

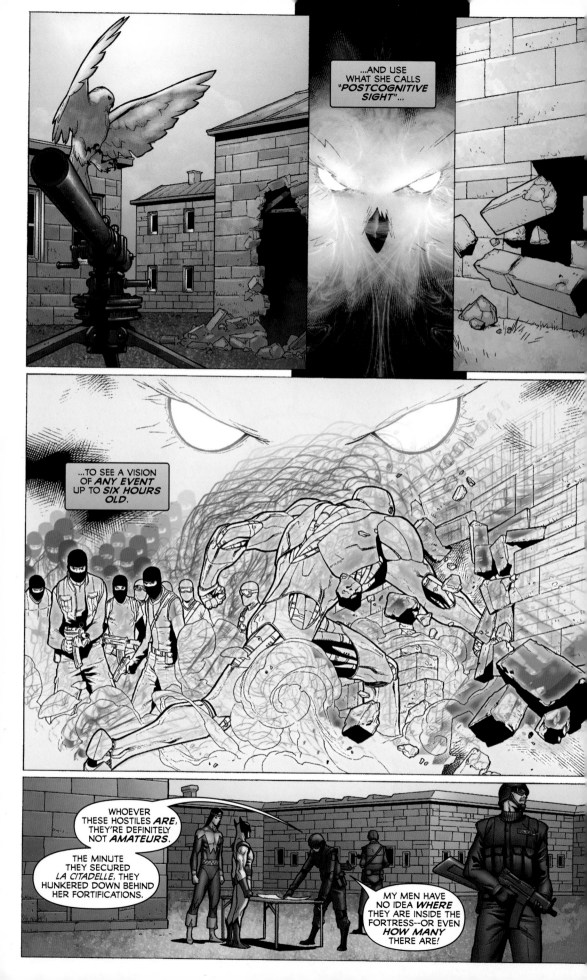

...AND USE WHAT SHE CALLS *"POSTCOGNITIVE SIGHT"*...

...TO SEE A VISION OF *ANY EVENT* UP TO *SIX HOURS OLD.*

WHOEVER THESE HOSTILES *ARE,* THEY'RE DEFINITELY NOT *AMATEURS.*

THE MINUTE THEY SECURED *LA CITADELLE,* THEY HUNKERED DOWN BEHIND HER FORTIFICATIONS.

MY MEN HAVE NO IDEA *WHERE* THEY ARE INSIDE THE FORTRESS--OR EVEN *HOW MANY* THERE ARE!

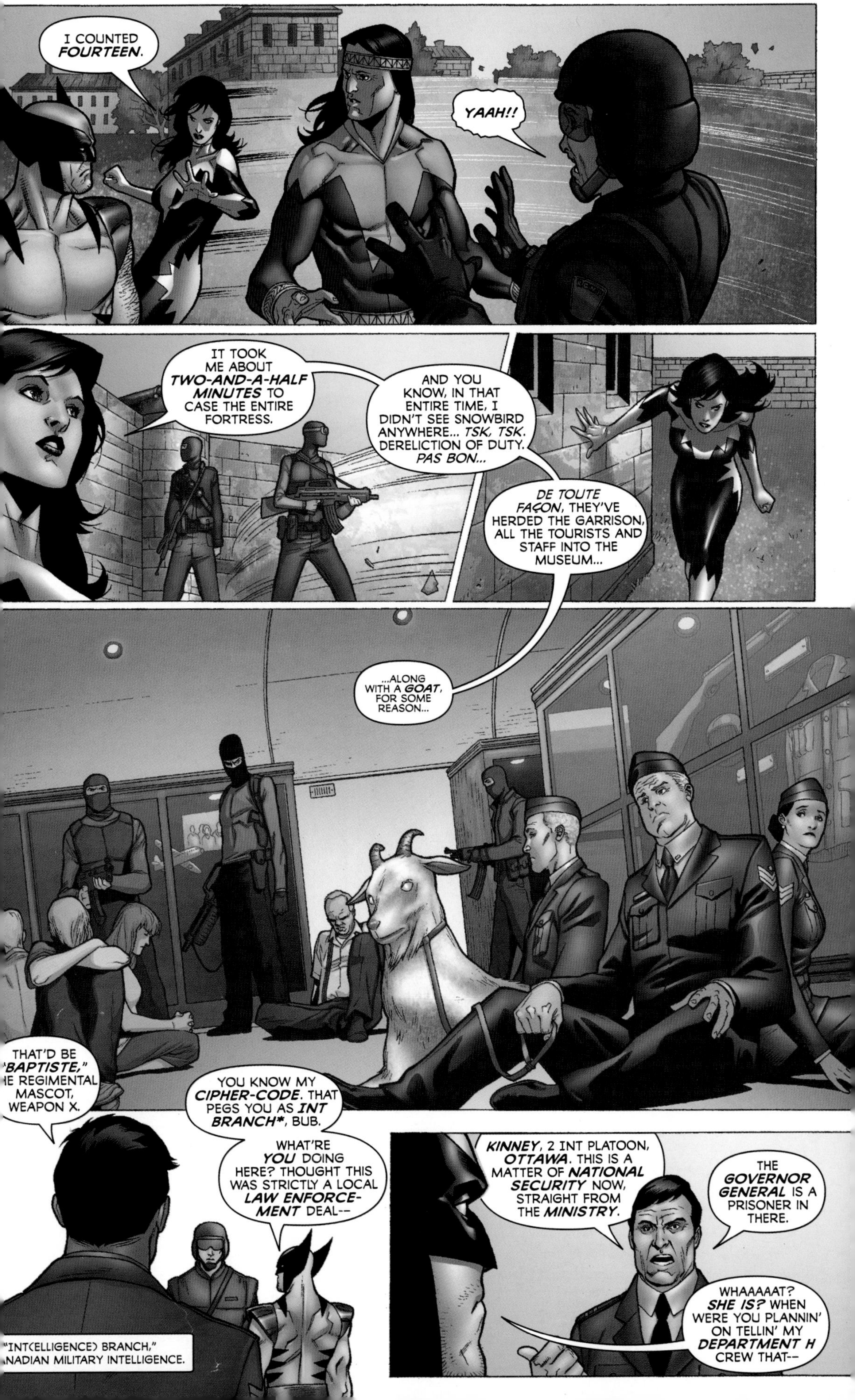

I COUNTED FOURTEEN.
YAAH!!
IT TOOK ME ABOUT TWO-AND-A-HALF MINUTES TO CASE THE ENTIRE FORTRESS.
AND YOU KNOW, IN THAT ENTIRE TIME, I DIDN'T SEE SNOWBIRD ANYWHERE... TSK, TSK. DERELICTION OF DUTY. PAS BON...
DE TOUTE FAÇON, THEY'VE HERDED THE GARRISON, ALL THE TOURISTS AND STAFF INTO THE MUSEUM...
...ALONG WITH A GOAT, FOR SOME REASON...
THAT'D BE "BAPTISTE," HE REGIMENTAL MASCOT, WEAPON X.
YOU KNOW MY CIPHER-CODE. THAT PEGS YOU AS INT BRANCH*, BUB.
WHAT'RE YOU DOING HERE? THOUGHT THIS WAS STRICTLY A LOCAL LAW ENFORCEMENT DEAL--
*INT(ELLIGENCE) BRANCH," NADIAN MILITARY INTELLIGENCE.
KINNEY, 2 INT PLATOON, OTTAWA. THIS IS A MATTER OF NATIONAL SECURITY NOW, STRAIGHT FROM THE MINISTRY.
THE GOVERNOR GENERAL IS A PRISONER IN THERE.
WHAAAAAT? SHE IS? WHEN WERE YOU PLANNIN' ON TELLIN' MY DEPARTMENT H CREW THAT--

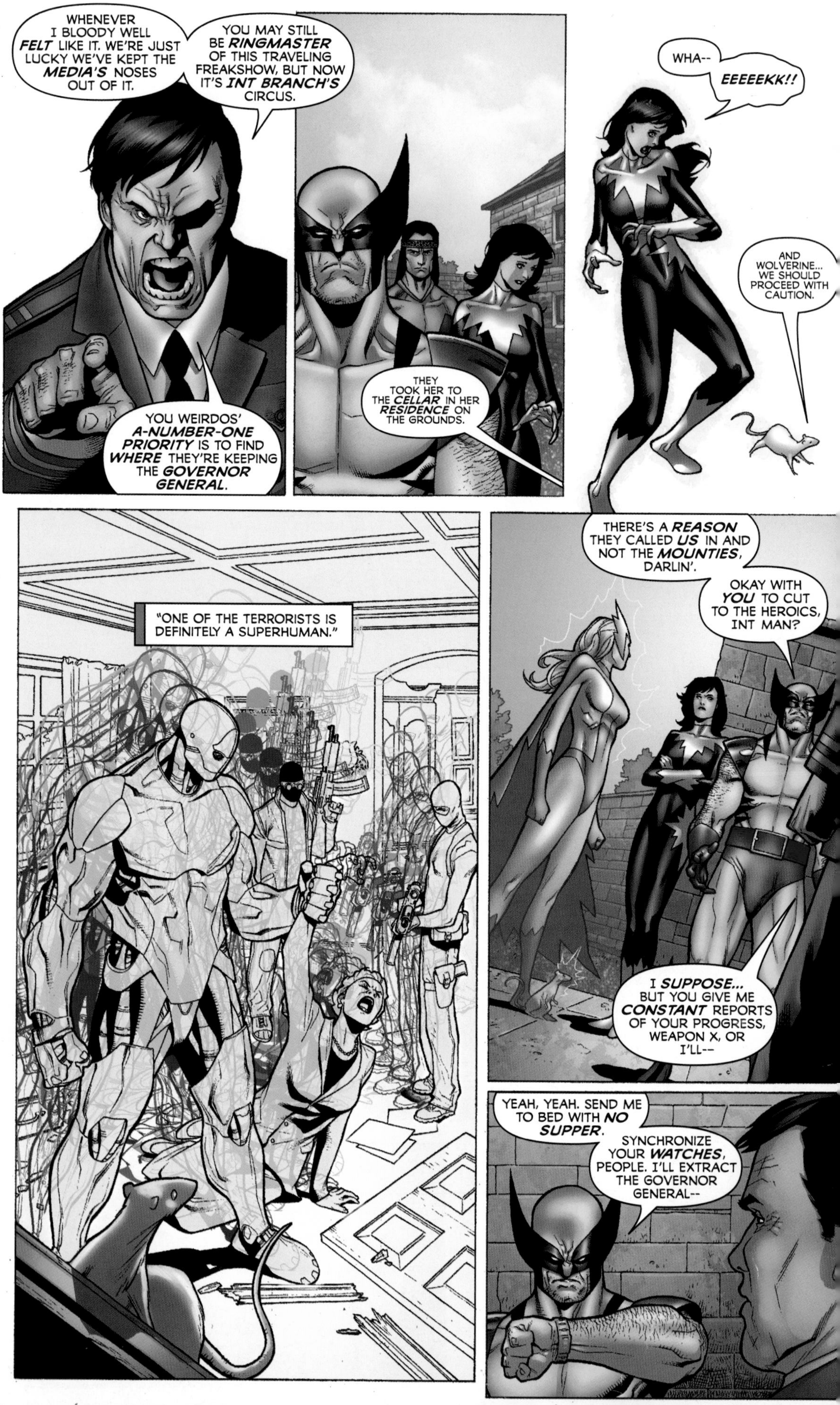

WHENEVER I BLOODY WELL FELT LIKE IT. WE'RE JUST LUCKY WE'VE KEPT THE MEDIA'S NOSES OUT OF IT.
YOU MAY STILL BE RINGMASTER OF THIS TRAVELING FREAKSHOW, BUT NOW IT'S INT BRANCH'S CIRCUS.
YOU WEIRDOS' A-NUMBER-ONE PRIORITY IS TO FIND WHERE THEY'RE KEEPING THE GOVERNOR GENERAL.
THEY TOOK HER TO THE CELLAR IN HER RESIDENCE ON THE GROUNDS.
WHA--
EEEEEKK!!
AND WOLVERINE... WE SHOULD PROCEED WITH CAUTION.
"ONE OF THE TERRORISTS IS DEFINITELY A SUPERHUMAN."
THERE'S A REASON THEY CALLED US IN AND NOT THE MOUNTIES, DARLIN'.
OKAY WITH YOU TO CUT TO THE HEROICS, INT MAN?
I SUPPOSE... BUT YOU GIVE ME CONSTANT REPORTS OF YOUR PROGRESS, WEAPON X, OR I'LL--
YEAH, YEAH. SEND ME TO BED WITH NO SUPPER.
SYNCHRONIZE YOUR WATCHES, PEOPLE. I'LL EXTRACT THE GOVERNOR GENERAL--

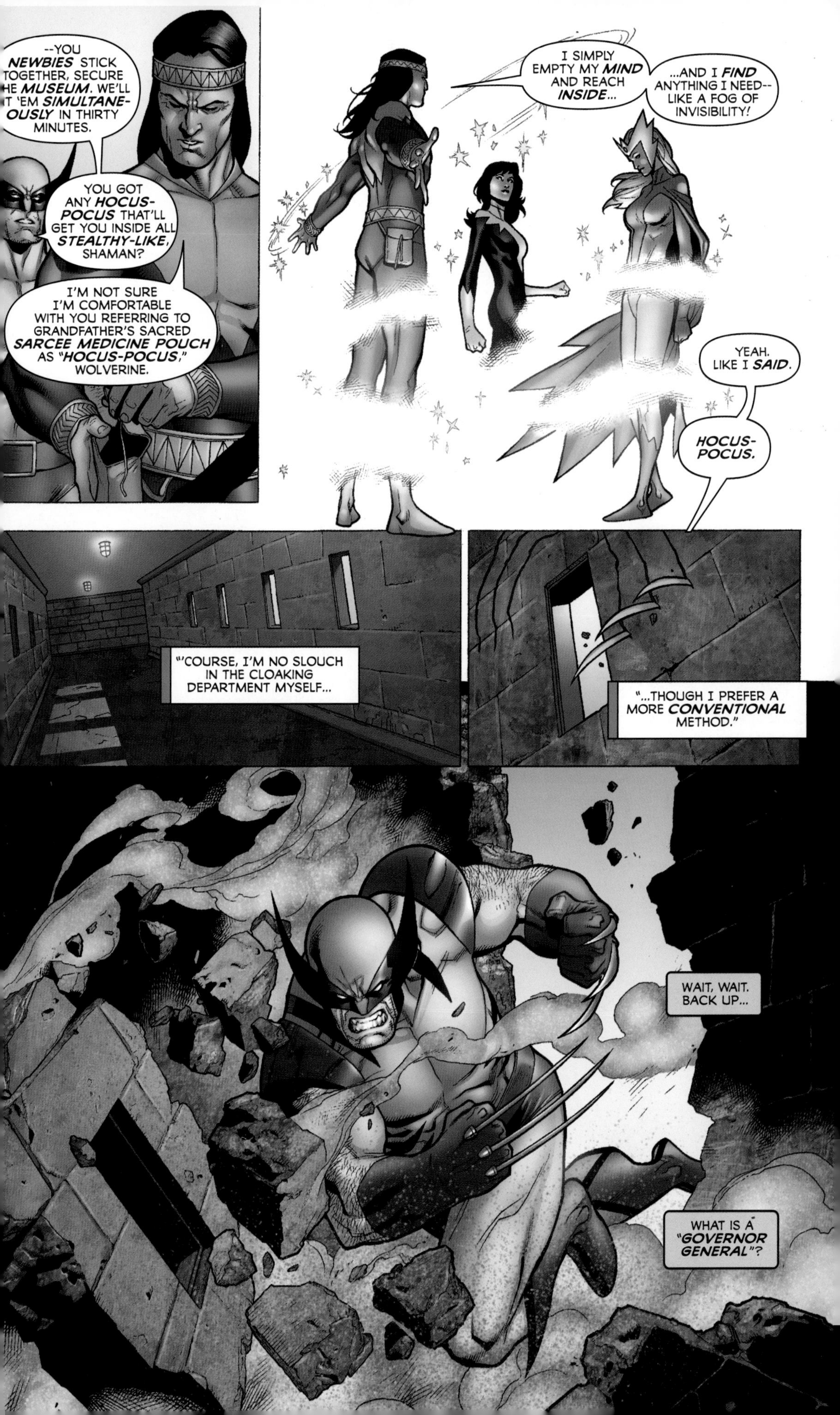
--YOU NEWBIES STICK TOGETHER, SECURE HE MUSEUM. WE'LL T 'EM SIMULTANEOUSLY IN THIRTY MINUTES.
YOU GOT ANY HOCUS-POCUS THAT'LL GET YOU INSIDE ALL STEALTHY-LIKE, SHAMAN?
I'M NOT SURE I'M COMFORTABLE WITH YOU REFERRING TO GRANDFATHER'S SACRED SARCEE MEDICINE POUCH AS "HOCUS-POCUS," WOLVERINE.
I SIMPLY EMPTY MY MIND AND REACH INSIDE...
...AND I FIND ANYTHING I NEED-- LIKE A FOG OF INVISIBILITY!
YEAH. LIKE I SAID.
HOCUS-POCUS.
"'COURSE, I'M NO SLOUCH IN THE CLOAKING DEPARTMENT MYSELF...
"...THOUGH I PREFER A MORE CONVENTIONAL METHOD."
WAIT, WAIT. BACK UP...
WHAT IS A "GOVERNOR GENERAL"?

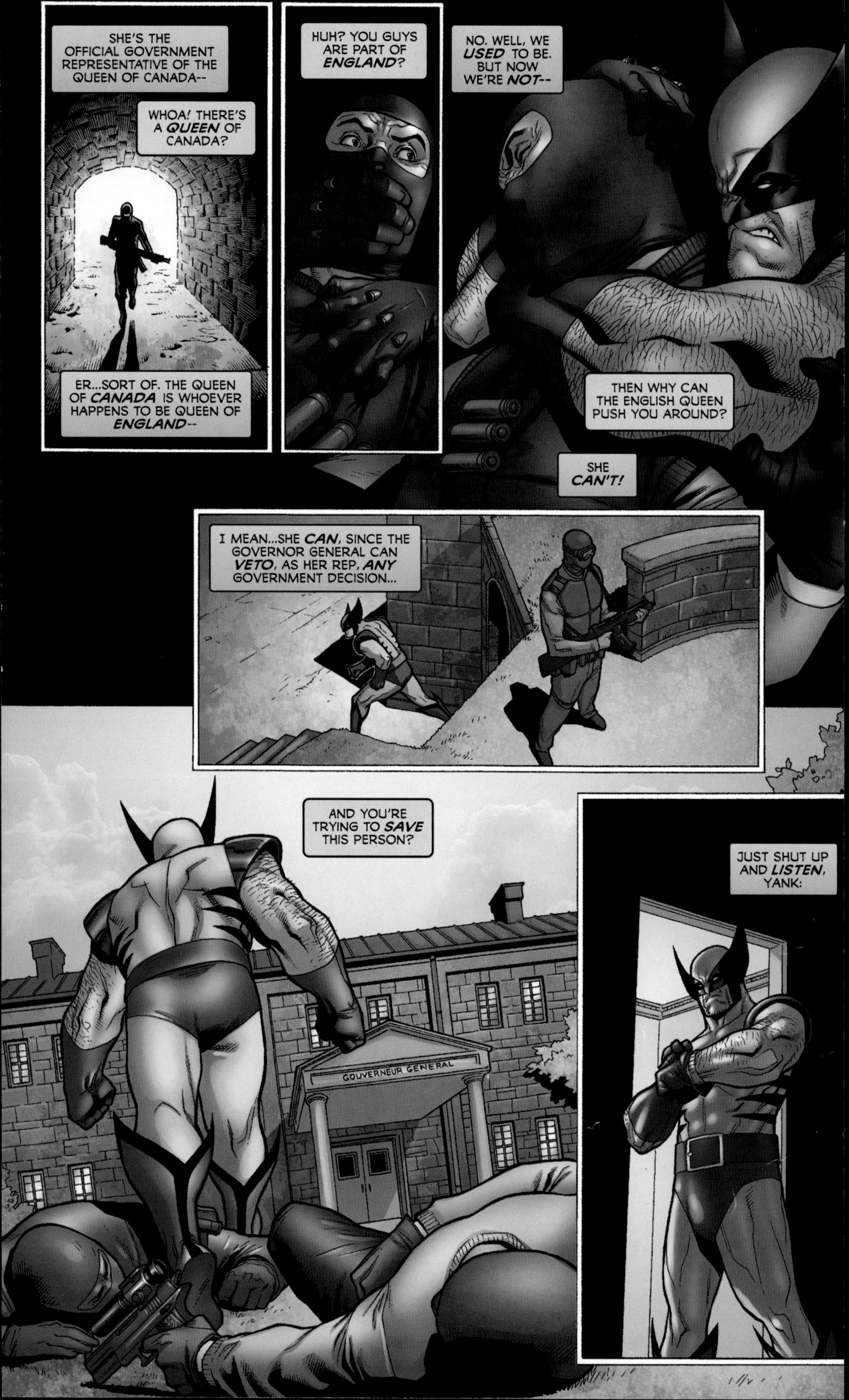

SHE'S THE OFFICIAL GOVERNMENT REPRESENTATIVE OF THE QUEEN OF CANADA--
WHOA! THERE'S A QUEEN OF CANADA?
ER...SORT OF. THE QUEEN OF CANADA IS WHOEVER HAPPENS TO BE QUEEN OF ENGLAND--
HUH? YOU GUYS ARE PART OF ENGLAND?
NO. WELL, WE USED TO BE. BUT NOW WE'RE NOT--
THEN WHY CAN THE ENGLISH QUEEN PUSH YOU AROUND?
SHE CAN'T!
I MEAN...SHE CAN, SINCE THE GOVERNOR GENERAL CAN VETO, AS HER REP, ANY GOVERNMENT DECISION...
AND YOU'RE TRYING TO SAVE THIS PERSON?
GOUVERNEUR GENERAL
JUST SHUT UP AND LISTEN, YANK:

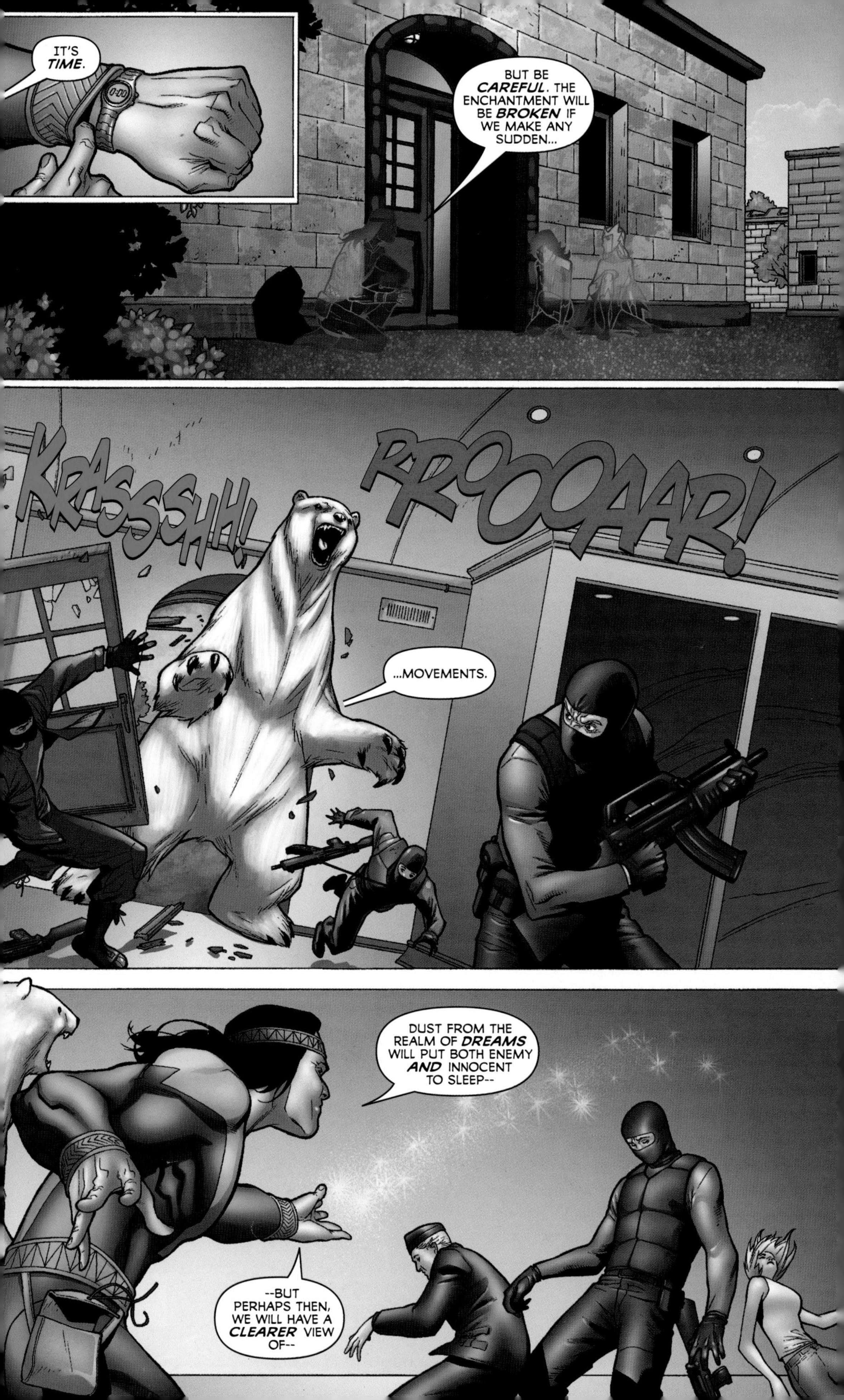
IT'S TIME.
BUT BE CAREFUL. THE ENCHANTMENT WILL BE BROKEN IF WE MAKE ANY SUDDEN...
KRASSSHH!
RROOOAAR!
...MOVEMENTS.
DUST FROM THE REALM OF DREAMS WILL PUT BOTH ENEMY AND INNOCENT TO SLEEP--
--BUT PERHAPS THEN, WE WILL HAVE A CLEARER VIEW OF--

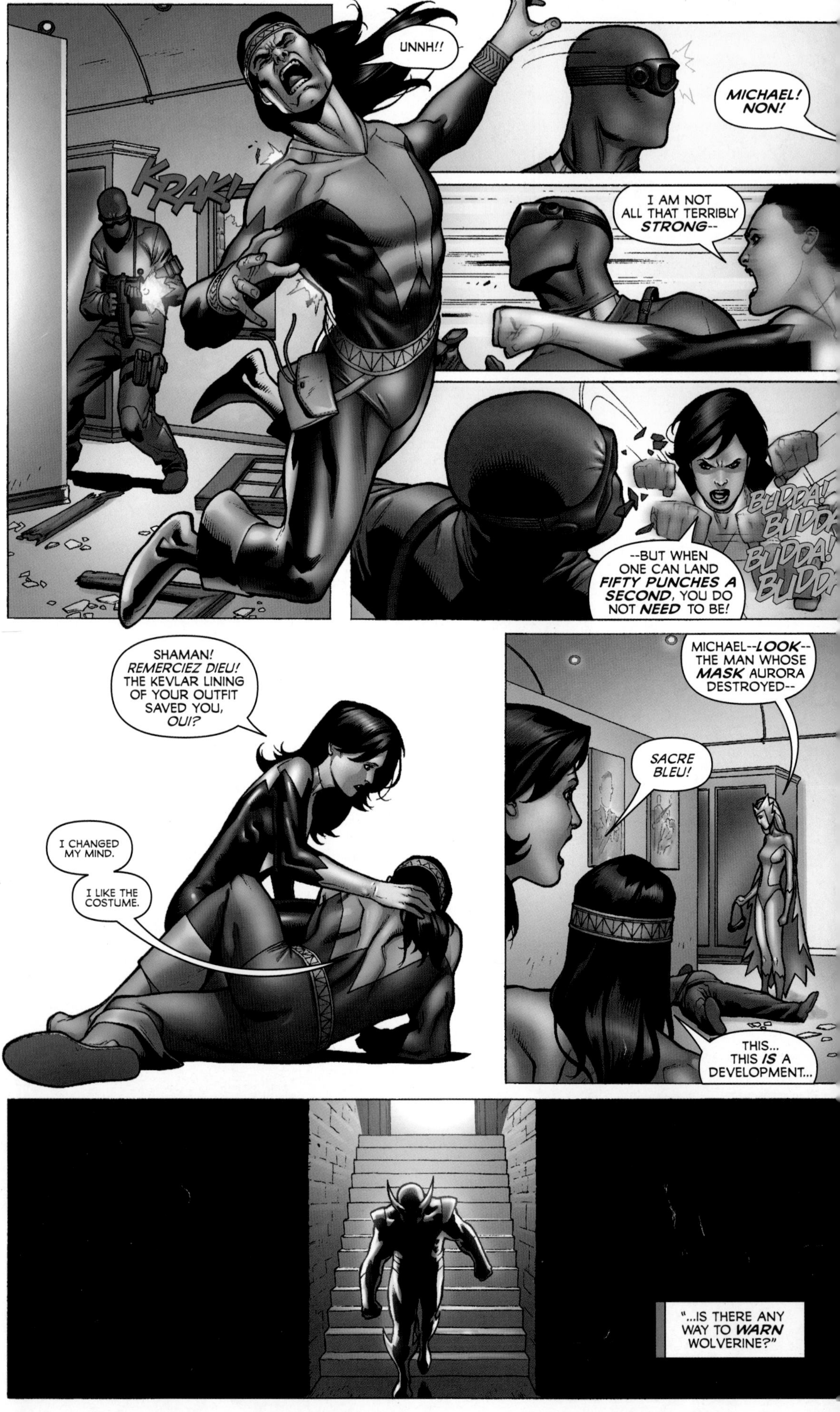

UNNH!!
MICHAEL! NON!
KRAK!
I AM NOT ALL THAT TERRIBLY STRONG--
--BUT WHEN ONE CAN LAND FIFTY PUNCHES A SECOND, YOU DO NOT NEED TO BE!
BUDDA! BUDDA! BUDDA! BUDDA!
SHAMAN! REMERCIEZ DIEU! THE KEVLAR LINING OF YOUR OUTFIT SAVED YOU, OUI?
I CHANGED MY MIND.
I LIKE THE COSTUME.
MICHAEL--LOOK-- THE MAN WHOSE MASK AURORA DESTROYED--
SACRE BLEU!
THIS... THIS IS A DEVELOPMENT...
"...IS THERE ANY WAY TO WARN WOLVERINE?"

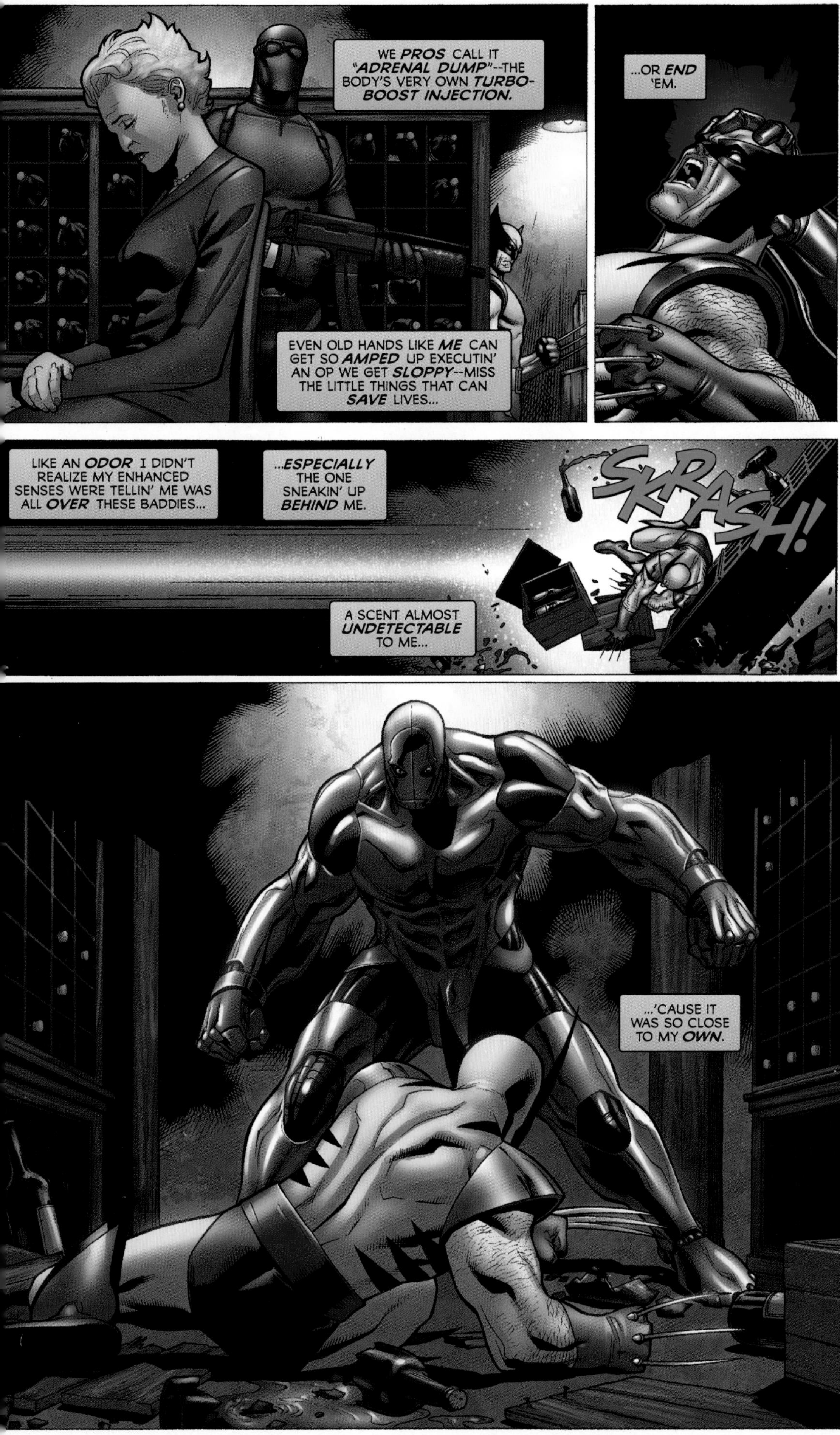
WE PROS CALL IT "ADRENAL DUMP"--THE BODY'S VERY OWN TURBO-BOOST INJECTION.
EVEN OLD HANDS LIKE ME CAN GET SO AMPED UP EXECUTIN' AN OP WE GET SLOPPY--MISS THE LITTLE THINGS THAT CAN SAVE LIVES...
...OR END 'EM.
LIKE AN ODOR I DIDN'T REALIZE MY ENHANCED SENSES WERE TELLIN' ME WAS ALL OVER THESE BADDIES...
...ESPECIALLY THE ONE SNEAKIN' UP BEHIND ME.
SKRASH!
A SCENT ALMOST UNDETECTABLE TO ME...
...'CAUSE IT WAS SO CLOSE TO MY OWN.

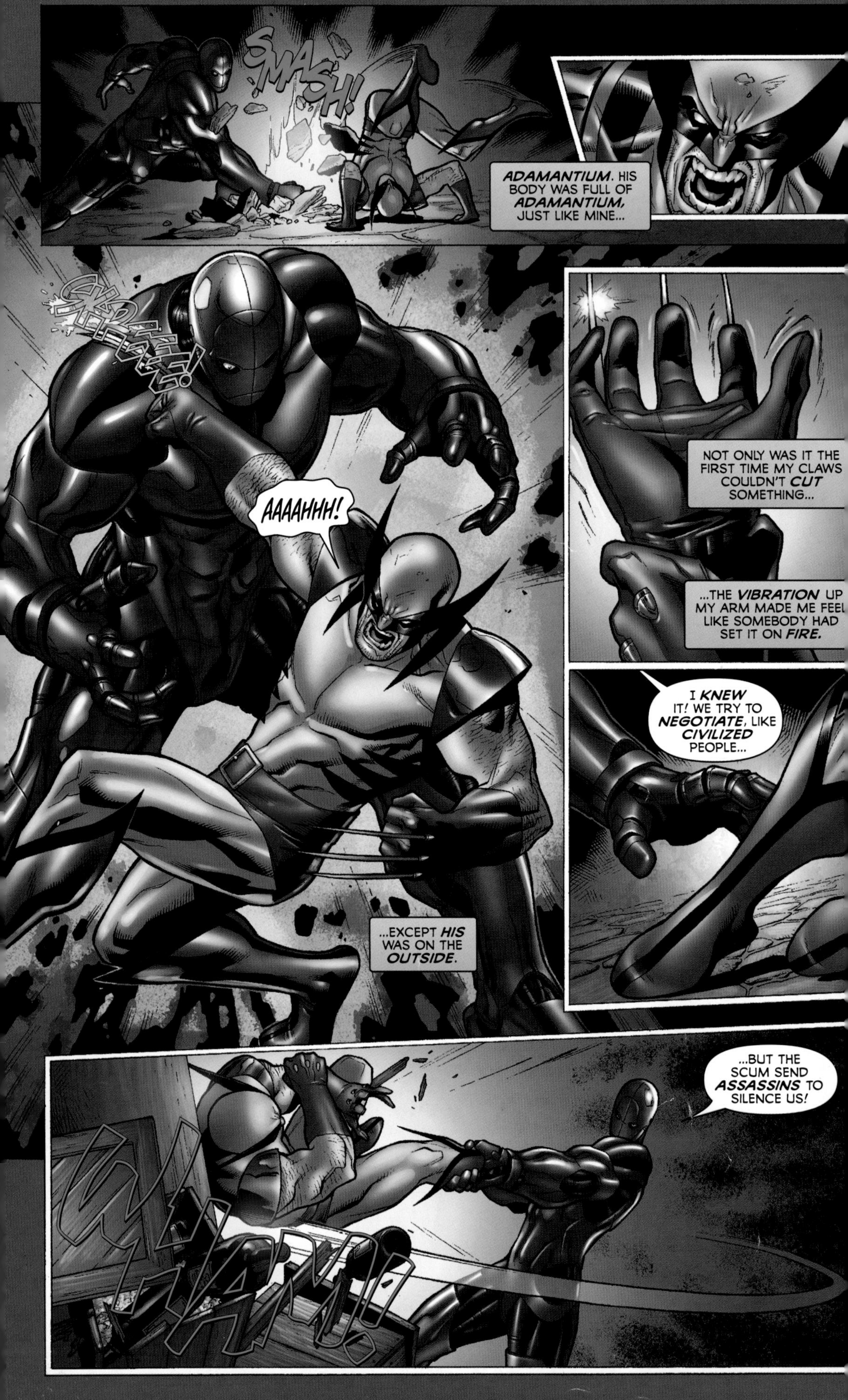
SMASH!
ADAMANTIUM. HIS BODY WAS FULL OF ADAMANTIUM, JUST LIKE MINE...
AAAAHHH!
...EXCEPT HIS WAS ON THE OUTSIDE.
NOT ONLY WAS IT THE FIRST TIME MY CLAWS COULDN'T CUT SOMETHING...
...THE VIBRATION UP MY ARM MADE ME FEEL LIKE SOMEBODY HAD SET IT ON FIRE.
I KNEW IT! WE TRY TO NEGOTIATE, LIKE CIVILIZED PEOPLE...
...BUT THE SCUM SEND ASSASSINS TO SILENCE US!

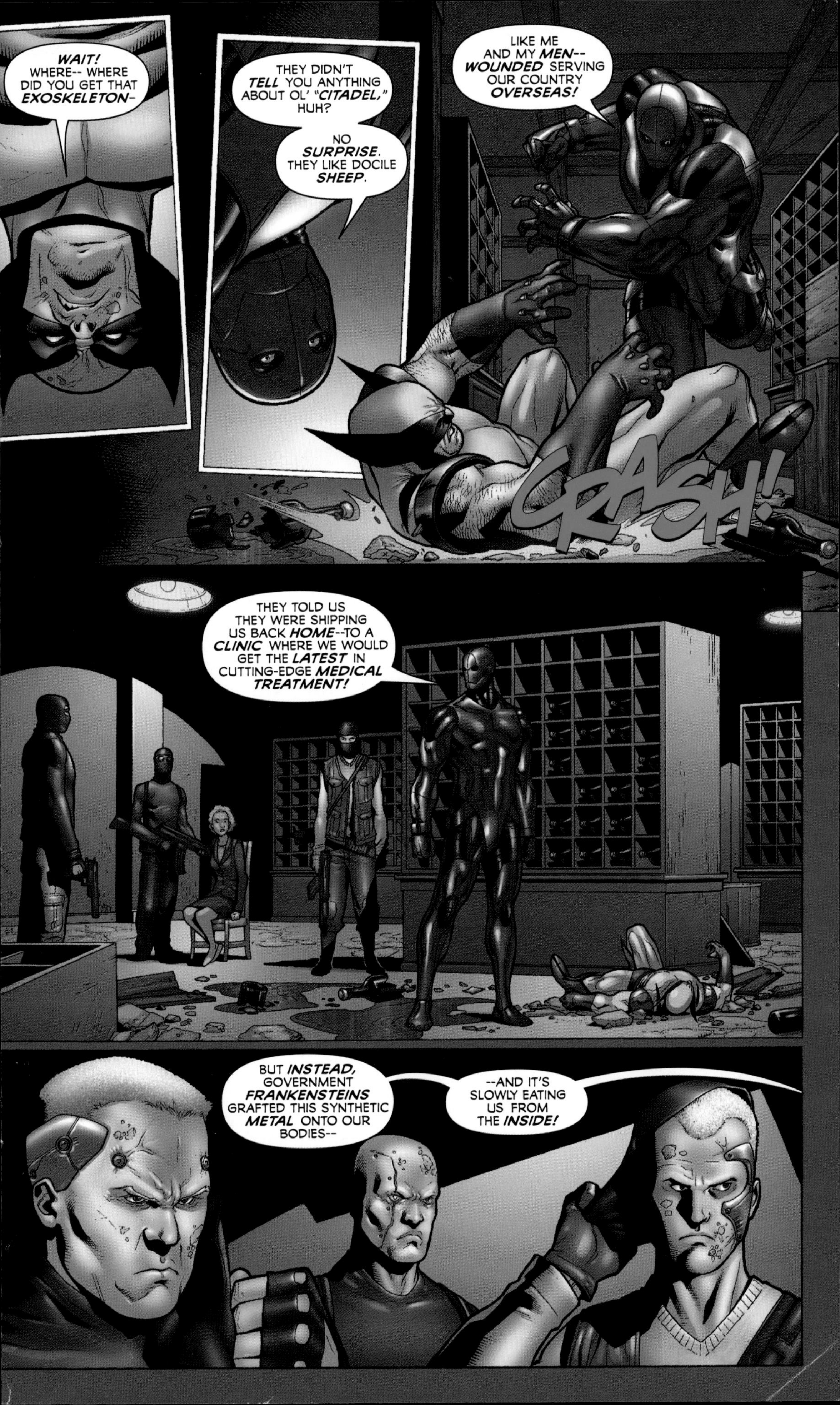
WAIT! WHERE-- WHERE DID YOU GET THAT EXOSKELETON-
THEY DIDN'T TELL YOU ANYTHING ABOUT OL' "CITADEL," HUH?
NO SURPRISE. THEY LIKE DOCILE SHEEP.
LIKE ME AND MY MEN--WOUNDED SERVING OUR COUNTRY OVERSEAS!
CRASH!
THEY TOLD US THEY WERE SHIPPING US BACK HOME--TO A CLINIC WHERE WE WOULD GET THE LATEST IN CUTTING-EDGE MEDICAL TREATMENT!
BUT INSTEAD, GOVERNMENT FRANKENSTEINS GRAFTED THIS SYNTHETIC METAL ONTO OUR BODIES--
--AND IT'S SLOWLY EATING US FROM THE INSIDE!

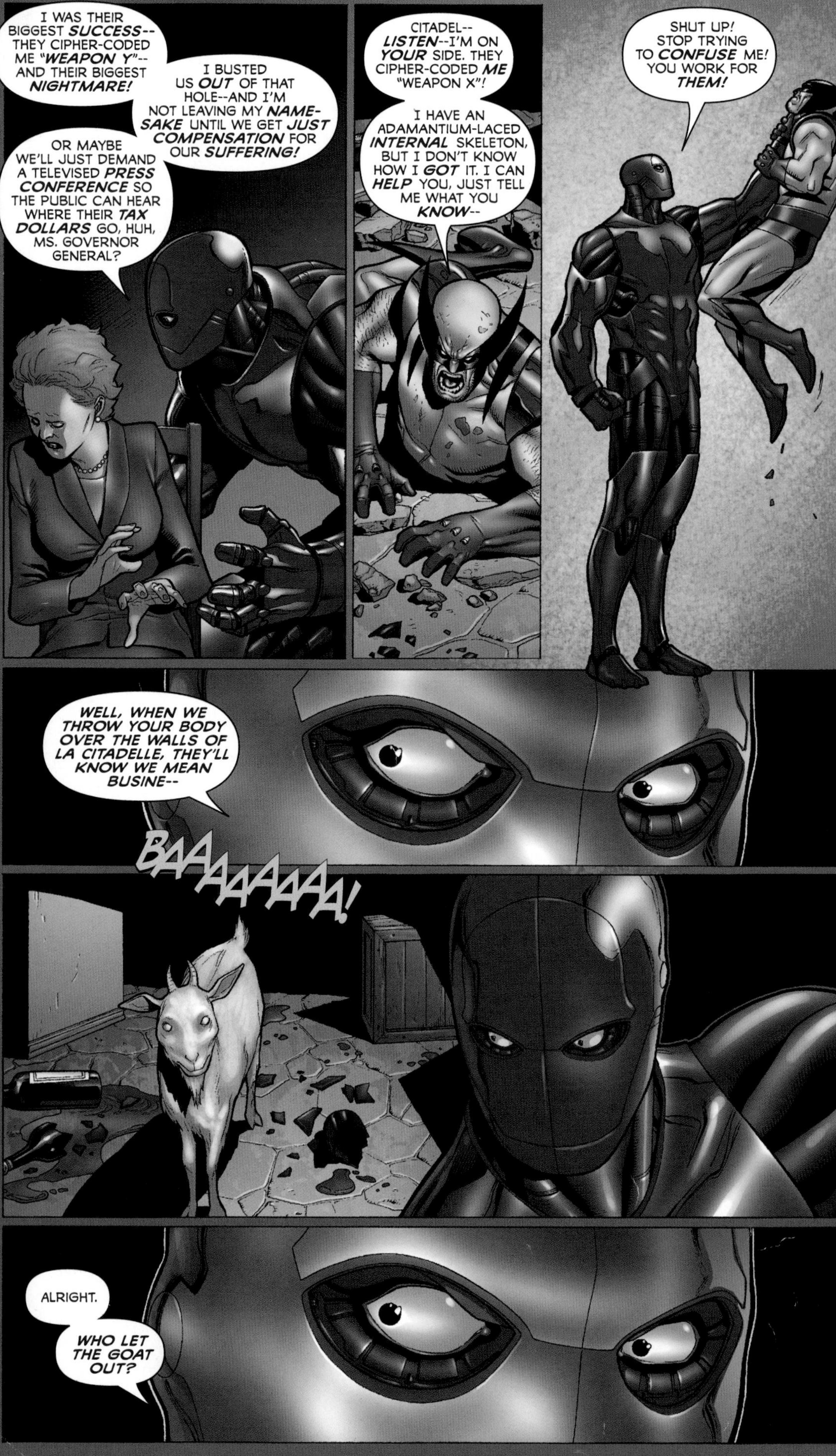

I WAS THEIR BIGGEST SUCCESS--THEY CIPHER-CODED ME "WEAPON Y"--AND THEIR BIGGEST NIGHTMARE!
I BUSTED US OUT OF THAT HOLE--AND I'M NOT LEAVING MY NAME-SAKE UNTIL WE GET JUST COMPENSATION FOR OUR SUFFERING!
OR MAYBE WE'LL JUST DEMAND A TELEVISED PRESS CONFERENCE SO THE PUBLIC CAN HEAR WHERE THEIR TAX DOLLARS GO, HUH, MS. GOVERNOR GENERAL?
CITADEL--LISTEN--I'M ON YOUR SIDE. THEY CIPHER-CODED ME "WEAPON X"!
I HAVE AN ADAMANTIUM-LACED INTERNAL SKELETON, BUT I DON'T KNOW HOW I GOT IT. I CAN HELP YOU, JUST TELL ME WHAT YOU KNOW--
SHUT UP! STOP TRYING TO CONFUSE ME! YOU WORK FOR THEM!
WELL, WHEN WE THROW YOUR BODY OVER THE WALLS OF LA CITADELLE, THEY'LL KNOW WE MEAN BUSINE--
BAAAAAAAA!
ALRIGHT.
WHO LET THE GOAT OUT?

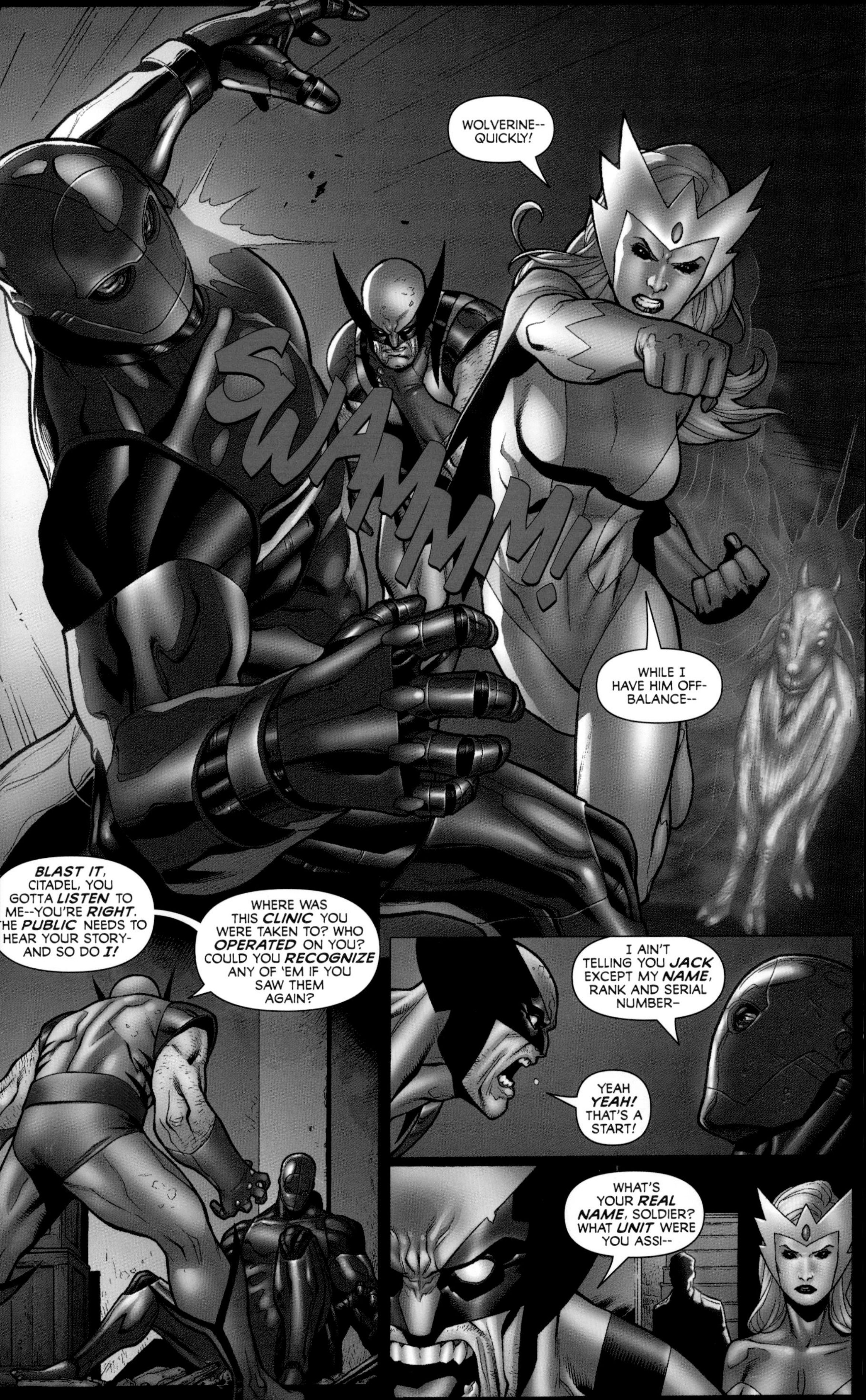

WOLVERINE-- QUICKLY!
SWAMMM!
WHILE I HAVE HIM OFF-BALANCE--
BLAST IT, CITADEL, YOU GOTTA LISTEN TO ME--YOU'RE RIGHT. THE PUBLIC NEEDS TO HEAR YOUR STORY- AND SO DO I!
WHERE WAS THIS CLINIC YOU WERE TAKEN TO? WHO OPERATED ON YOU? COULD YOU RECOGNIZE ANY OF 'EM IF YOU SAW THEM AGAIN?
I AIN'T TELLING YOU JACK EXCEPT MY NAME, RANK AND SERIAL NUMBER–
YEAH YEAH! THAT'S A START!
WHAT'S YOUR REAL NAME, SOLDIER? WHAT UNIT WERE YOU ASSI--

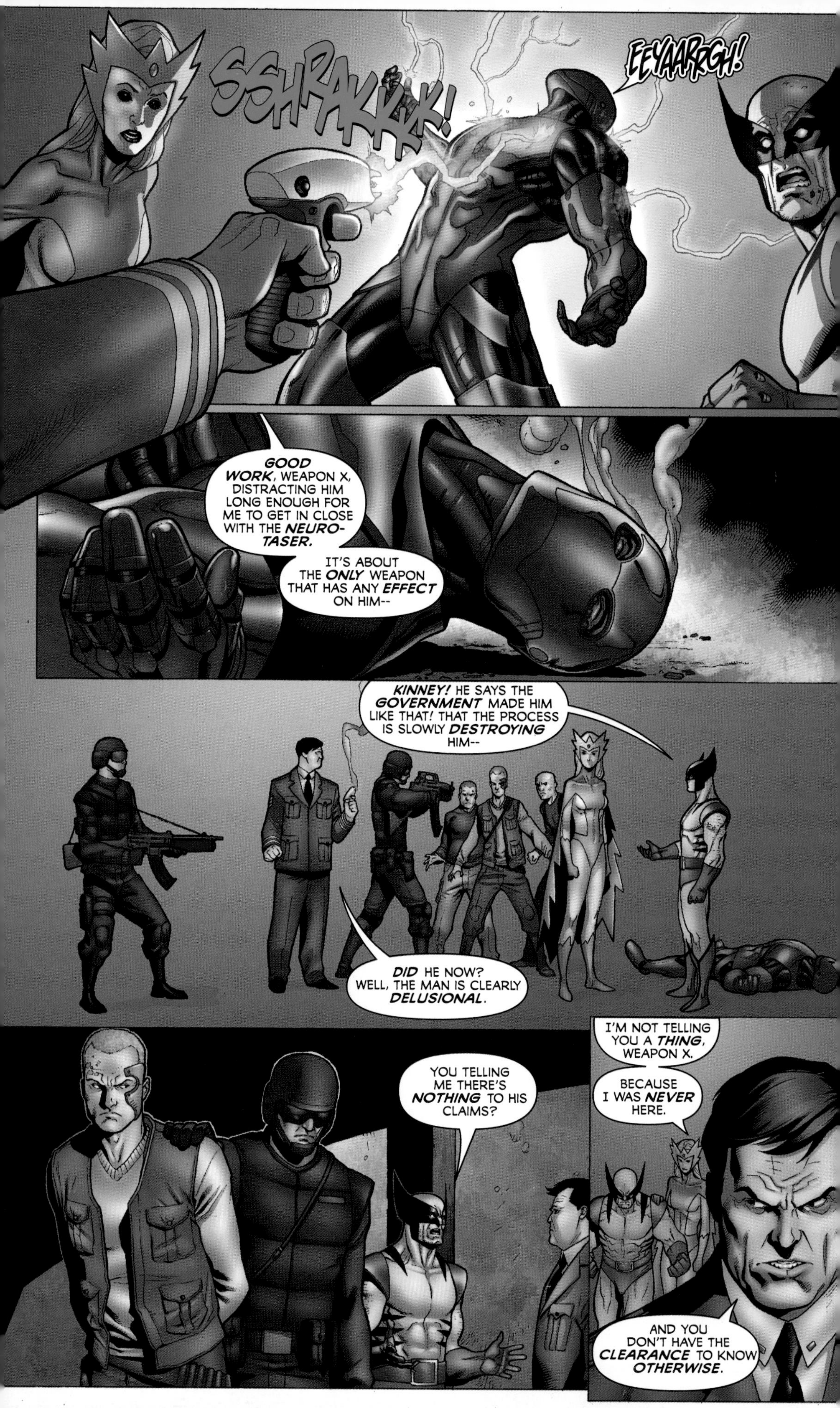
SSHRAKKK!
EEYAARRGH!
GOOD WORK, WEAPON X, DISTRACTING HIM LONG ENOUGH FOR ME TO GET IN CLOSE WITH THE NEURO-TASER.
IT'S ABOUT THE ONLY WEAPON THAT HAS ANY EFFECT ON HIM--
KINNEY! HE SAYS THE GOVERNMENT MADE HIM LIKE THAT! THAT THE PROCESS IS SLOWLY DESTROYING HIM--
DID HE NOW? WELL, THE MAN IS CLEARLY DELUSIONAL.
YOU TELLING ME THERE'S NOTHING TO HIS CLAIMS?
I'M NOT TELLING YOU A THING, WEAPON X.
BECAUSE I WAS NEVER HERE.
AND YOU DON'T HAVE THE CLEARANCE TO KNOW OTHERWISE.

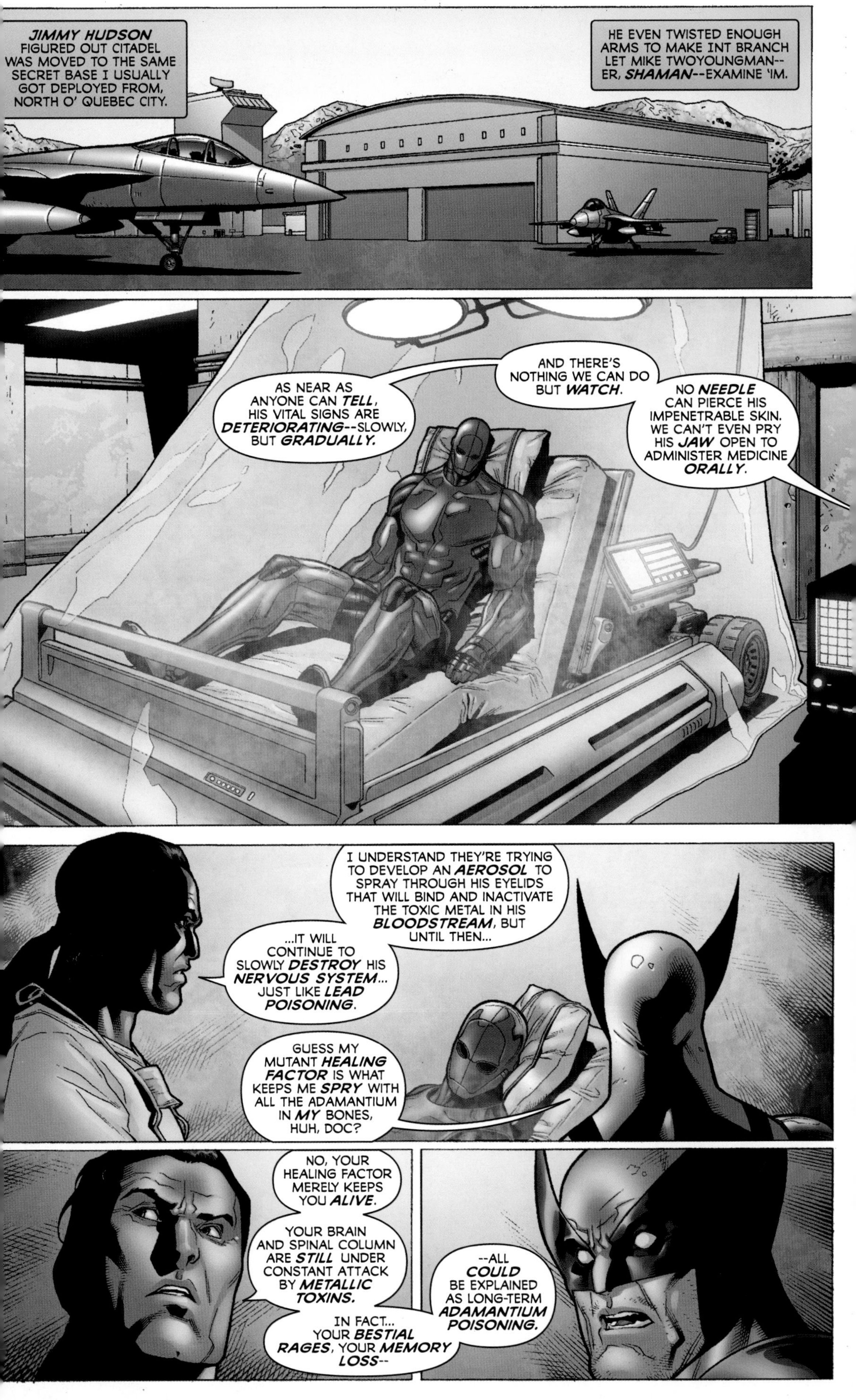
JIMMY HUDSON FIGURED OUT CITADEL WAS MOVED TO THE SAME SECRET BASE I USUALLY GOT DEPLOYED FROM, NORTH O' QUEBEC CITY.
HE EVEN TWISTED ENOUGH ARMS TO MAKE INT BRANCH LET MIKE TWOYOUNGMAN--ER, SHAMAN--EXAMINE 'IM.
AS NEAR AS ANYONE CAN TELL, HIS VITAL SIGNS ARE DETERIORATING--SLOWLY, BUT GRADUALLY.
AND THERE'S NOTHING WE CAN DO BUT WATCH.
NO NEEDLE CAN PIERCE HIS IMPENETRABLE SKIN. WE CAN'T EVEN PRY HIS JAW OPEN TO ADMINISTER MEDICINE ORALLY.
I UNDERSTAND THEY'RE TRYING TO DEVELOP AN AEROSOL TO SPRAY THROUGH HIS EYELIDS THAT WILL BIND AND INACTIVATE THE TOXIC METAL IN HIS BLOODSTREAM, BUT UNTIL THEN...
...IT WILL CONTINUE TO SLOWLY DESTROY HIS NERVOUS SYSTEM... JUST LIKE LEAD POISONING.
GUESS MY MUTANT HEALING FACTOR IS WHAT KEEPS ME SPRY WITH ALL THE ADAMANTIUM IN MY BONES, HUH, DOC?
NO, YOUR HEALING FACTOR MERELY KEEPS YOU ALIVE.
YOUR BRAIN AND SPINAL COLUMN ARE STILL UNDER CONSTANT ATTACK BY METALLIC TOXINS.
IN FACT... YOUR BESTIAL RAGES, YOUR MEMORY LOSS--
--ALL COULD BE EXPLAINED AS LONG-TERM ADAMANTIUM POISONING.

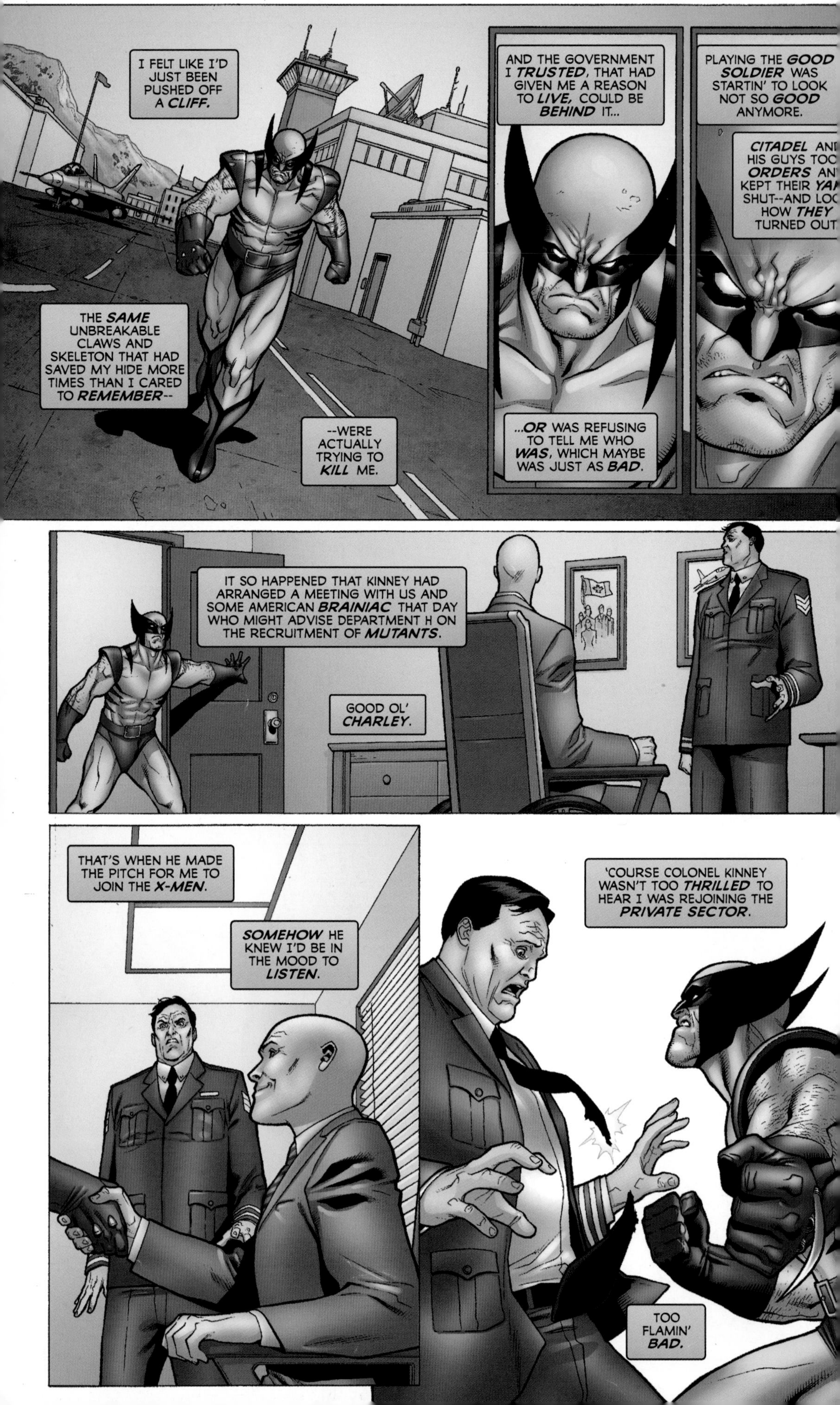

I FELT LIKE I'D JUST BEEN PUSHED OFF A CLIFF.
THE SAME UNBREAKABLE CLAWS AND SKELETON THAT HAD SAVED MY HIDE MORE TIMES THAN I CARED TO REMEMBER--
--WERE ACTUALLY TRYING TO KILL ME.
AND THE GOVERNMENT I TRUSTED, THAT HAD GIVEN ME A REASON TO LIVE, COULD BE BEHIND IT...
...OR WAS REFUSING TO TELL ME WHO WAS, WHICH MAYBE WAS JUST AS BAD.
PLAYING THE GOOD SOLDIER WAS STARTIN' TO LOOK NOT SO GOOD ANYMORE.
IT SO HAPPENED THAT KINNEY HAD ARRANGED A MEETING WITH US AND SOME AMERICAN BRAINIAC THAT DAY WHO MIGHT ADVISE DEPARTMENT H ON THE RECRUITMENT OF MUTANTS.
GOOD OL' CHARLEY.
THAT'S WHEN HE MADE THE PITCH FOR ME TO JOIN THE X-MEN.
SOMEHOW HE KNEW I'D BE IN THE MOOD TO LISTEN.
'COURSE COLONEL KINNEY WASN'T TOO THRILLED TO HEAR I WAS REJOINING THE PRIVATE SECTOR.
TOO FLAMIN' BAD.

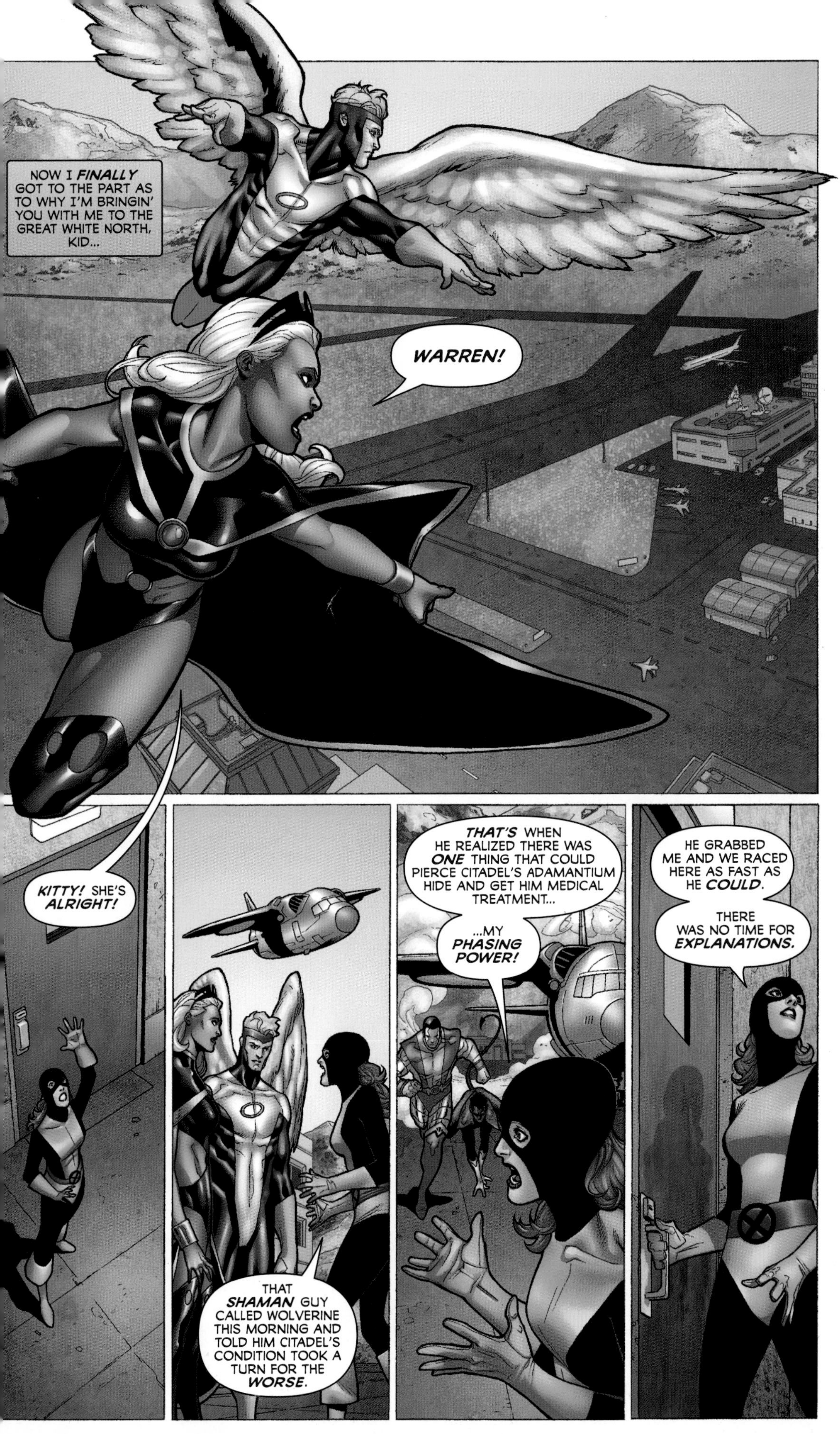
NOW I FINALLY GOT TO THE PART AS TO WHY I'M BRINGIN' YOU WITH ME TO THE GREAT WHITE NORTH, KID...
WARREN!
KITTY! SHE'S ALRIGHT!
THAT SHAMAN GUY CALLED WOLVERINE THIS MORNING AND TOLD HIM CITADEL'S CONDITION TOOK A TURN FOR THE WORSE.
THAT'S WHEN HE REALIZED THERE WAS ONE THING THAT COULD PIERCE CITADEL'S ADAMANTIUM HIDE AND GET HIM MEDICAL TREATMENT...
...MY PHASING POWER!
HE GRABBED ME AND WE RACED HERE AS FAST AS HE COULD.
THERE WAS NO TIME FOR EXPLANATIONS.

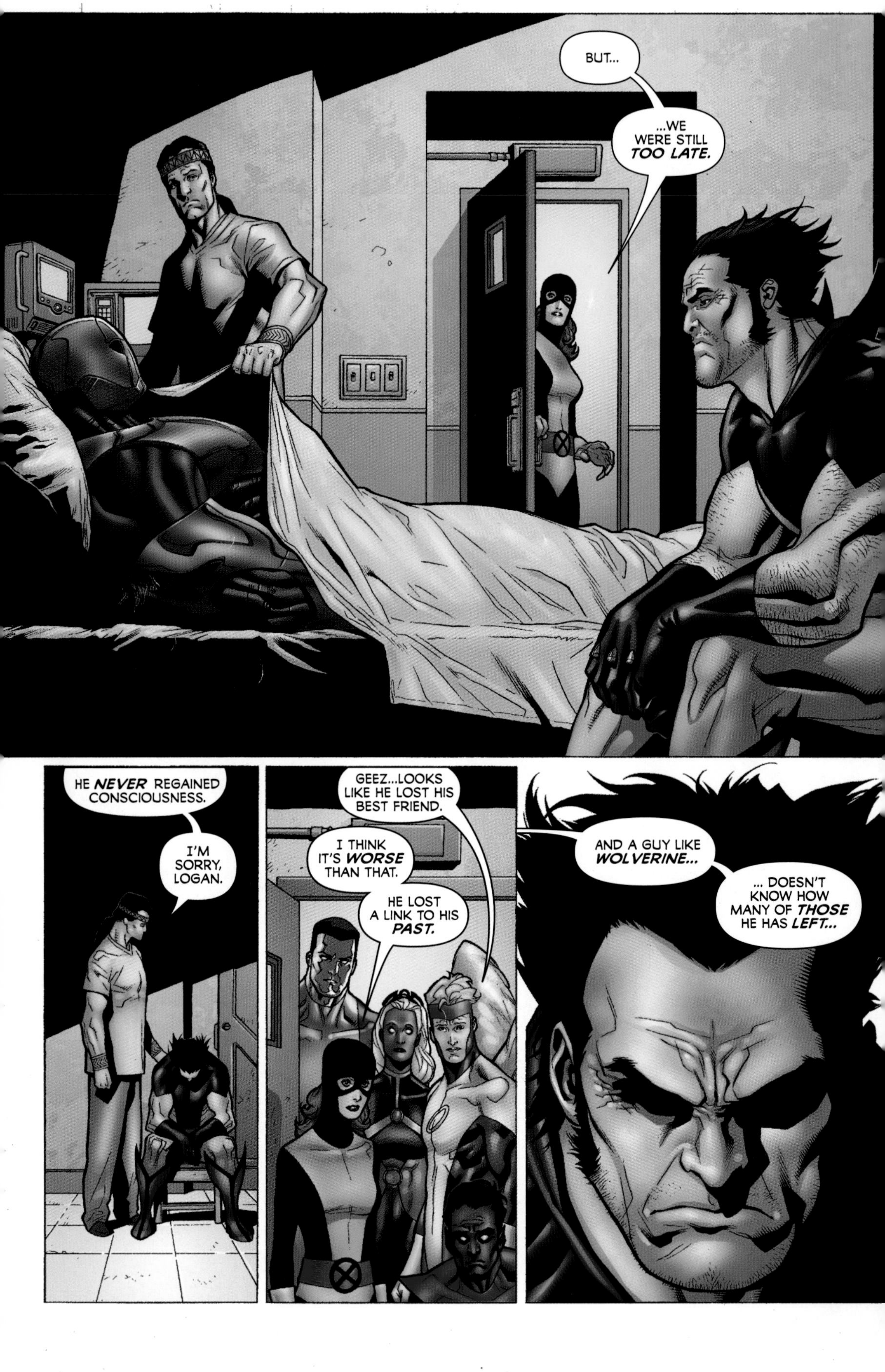
BUT...
...WE WERE STILL TOO LATE.
HE NEVER REGAINED CONSCIOUSNESS.
I'M SORRY, LOGAN.
GEEZ...LOOKS LIKE HE LOST HIS BEST FRIEND.
I THINK IT'S WORSE THAN THAT.
HE LOST A LINK TO HIS PAST.
AND A GUY LIKE WOLVERINE...
... DOESN'T KNOW HOW MANY OF THOSE HE HAS LEFT...